KEISHA THE FAIRY SNOW QUEEN

by Teresa Reed

Illustrations by
Eric Velasquez

Spot Illustrations by
Rich Grote

MAGIC ATTIC PRESS

For more information contact:
Book Editor, Magic Attic Press, 866 Spring Street,
P.O. Box 9722, Portland, ME 04104-5022.

First Edition
Printed in the United States of America
1 2 3 4 5 6 7 8 9 10

Magic Attic Club is a registered trademark of Magic Attic Press.

Betsy Gould, Editorial Director
Marva Martin, Art Director
Robin Haywood, Managing Editor

Edited by Judit Bodnar
Designed by Susi Oberhelman

ISBN 1-57513-024-6

Magic Attic Club books are printed on acid-free, recycled paper.

As members of the
MAGIC ATTIC CLUB,
we promise to
be best friends,
share all of our adventures in the attic,
use our imaginations,
have lots of fun together,
and remember—the real magic is in us.

Alison   *Keisha*

Heather   *Megan*

Table of Contents

THE
INCIDENT

A re you guys ready to go outside?" asked Keisha Vance as she buttoned up her brother's and sister's jackets and handed each of them a cookie.

"Yes, we're ready, Keisha," five-year-old Ashley exclaimed. The purple beads in her braids bounced as she jumped up and down. Ronnie, who was two, copied her words and movements exactly.

Keisha pulled Ashley's yellow knit hat over the tiny braids and tucked the matching muffler into her jacket.

"Listen," she said. "Keep an eye on Ronnie. Make sure he stays out of Dad's garden."

"No garden, Kee-kee, I *prombise*," boasted Ronnie, tugging his cap over his eyes. Keisha pulled it up so he could see, and he immediately yanked it back down. Keisha grinned as she readjusted it and wound his scarf around his neck. She'd barely finished when Ashley pulled the door open and the two little ones tumbled out into the backyard.

Every Wednesday and Thursday, Keisha had to hurry home from school to baby-sit her brother and sister while their parents worked at the hospital. Mrs. Vance was a nurse, and on those days she worked a double shift in the delivery ward. Mr. Vance was an administrator, so he was usually home by five-thirty. Sometimes Keisha wished that she could just come home and do anything she wanted, but deep down she didn't mind taking care of Ashley and Ronnie. They were really sweet, and the three of them usually had a lot of fun together.

Today, though, something awful had happened at school and she needed to talk to her three best friends. Even though they were all in the same class, she didn't know if the others had seen it, and right now she wanted their advice.

She picked up the phone and called her father's office.

"Hi, Daddy, it's Keisha," she said when his assistant got him on the line. "No, everything's fine. They're playing hide and seek in the backyard . . ." She moved to the sink and pushed aside the blue print curtains. Ashley and Ronnie were rolling on the ground and laughing.

"Daddy, may I invite Alison, Heather, and Megan over for a little while? . . .Thanks. Yes, I found the cookies that Mom made. I promise we won't spoil our dinner . . . Okay, Dad. I'll see you soon." Keisha took another look out the window as she dialed Alison's number. But her mind was on the Magic Attic Club, not on Ronnie and Ashley.

Keisha and her friends had met Alison's next-door neighbor, Ellie Goodwin, during their winter vacation from school. Ellie's attic was filled with treasures from her travels around the world: stacks of letters and old photographs, lovely holiday decorations, delicate figurines, and vases. Best of all were the tall, gilt-edged mirror and the old steamer trunk filled to the brim with every imaginable kind of outfit—and the amazing adventures the girls had whenever they tried one on and stood before the mirror.

It wasn't long before Megan Ryder, Alison McCann, and Heather Hardin—the other members of the Magic Attic Club—burst through the front door.

"I was in the middle of rereading A Wrinkle in Time," said Megan. The book was still in her hand. "What's up?"

"Yeah, why the urgent call, Keish?" asked Alison. "You sounded upset."

Heather squeezed past Alison. "I looked for you after school, but then I remembered that today's a baby-sitting day. Is something wrong with the kids?"

"No, everything on the home front is fine," said Keisha as the girls seated themselves around the kitchen table. She set a plate of peanut butter cookies and a stack of paper napkins in the middle and went to the cupboard for glasses. Megan jumped up and brought a jug of milk

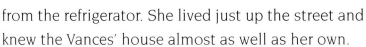

from the refrigerator. She lived just up the street and knew the Vances' house almost as well as her own.

"But the weirdest thing happened during our math quiz this afternoon," Keisha continued. "Did any of you see it?"

All the girls spoke at once. "No. What was it?" "Tell us, Keisha." "What happened?"

"Deanna cheated on the test!" Keisha exclaimed. There. She had finally gotten it off her chest.

Alison bit into a cookie and stared at Keisha. "Deanna's one of the smartest and most popular kids in class, maybe in the whole school. Are you sure she was cheating?"

"Well, I saw her take two notes from William, that new red-haired kid who sits next to her."

Heather gathered her long brown hair into a ponytail. "Maybe they were writing something about getting together after school. Lots of kids pass notes like that."

"But I saw her read the notes and then write something on her test paper," protested Keisha.

Megan wondered whether anyone else had seen them, and Keisha explained that when Deanna had finished copying from William's notes, she had looked around the room. She saw Keisha watching her and turned right back to her test without looking Keisha in the eye. When Keisha had checked around the classroom, everyone seemed to be concentrating on the test. Even Ms. Joseph, who came in several times a week to teach Science, Math, and Spanish, was busy correcting papers. It seemed that Keisha was the only one who knew what had happened, and she wasn't sure what to do about it.

"Keish, I don't think there's anything you can do. You don't want to tattle on anybody," said Alison.

"That's right," said Heather, nodding. "It's too late to do anything now, and it's not like you could have said anything to Ms. Joseph during the test."

"But she has to do something," cried Megan. "Cheating is cheating and it's wrong!"

Keisha rested her chin on her hands and stared at her cookie. "I don't think Deanna or William would admit they were cheating, do you? It would be their word against mine. But it makes me so mad! I studied really hard for that test, and Deanna's getting her grade for free!"

Megan nodded in agreement. "I studied a lot, too, Keisha. You've got to say something to Ms. Joseph. If you want, we could go see her together."

"What if Deanna tells everyone you ratted on her?" said Heather. "You don't want people saying mean things behind your back. Maybe you should just forget the whole thing." She glanced at Alison, who was the class president.

"I don't know," Alison said thoughtfully. "You didn't actually see what was in the note, did you?"

Keisha bit her lip. "Well, no, I didn't. But I know cheating when I see it." She looked up. "Megan . . . ?"

"Maybe Ali's right," replied Megan. "If you didn't see what was in the note, how can you be sure?"

Suddenly the kitchen door flew open and crashed against the counter, and the four girls jumped. There stood Ashley and Ronnie, peering around the door frame. Ashley looked up at Keisha with a worried expression.

"Are you going to tell on the cheaters, Keisha?" Ashley asked in a small voice.

Chapter

Two

SSHH! DON'T TELL

D on't worry about that right now, Ashley. You guys come inside and we'll start dinner. Daddy will be home any minute." Ashley and Ronnie ran in to hug Keisha's friends.

"Hi, Ash. Hi, Ronnie-o," said Megan, giving Ashley's yellow muffler an affectionate tug. "I have to go now, Keisha, but remember, I'm on your side."

"Thanks," said Keisha with a sigh. "That's good to know, Megan."

Alison pulled Ronnie's cap over his eyes and began swinging him by the hands. "It's a tough decision, Keish."

"I've got to go, too," said Heather as she put her arms around Keisha's shoulders. "My dad flew in this morning from Paris and I'm dying to see him. He was asleep when I got home from school."

"Paris? Neat! Say hi for me, will you?"

"Let us know what you decide," said Megan.

"Sure. Bye, everybody—and thanks," called Keisha as she closed the door behind her friends. She helped Ashley and Ronnie take off their jackets, then went to the den for paper and crayons for Ronnie. She found Ashley's favorite doll behind the couch and quickly got the children settled at the kitchen table. Then she washed a head of lettuce and a few tomatoes to start the dinner salad.

"Keisha?" said Ashley in a high-pitched voice. She held the little brown-skinned doll in her hands and walked her along the edge of the table.

"Hmm?"

"*Are* you going to tell on the bad kids who cheated?"

"Ashley! You know you shouldn't listen in on other people's conversations!"

"I couldn't help it. Are you going to tell? Mama says it's wrong to cheat."

"I know what Mama says, and she's right about that. But you see, Ashley, it's also not a good thing to tattle on someone else."

"Are you tattling if it's about something really bad?"

Keisha brought the cutting board and knife to the table and sat down. She tore lettuce into a bowl and chopped the tomatoes while she talked. She reminded Ashley of the time she had tripped as she ran in the living room and had knocked over their mother's good blue glass vase. It had broken into many little pieces.

"I remember," said Ashley with a little frown. "I was really upset, but you didn't tell on me."

"That's right," Keisha replied. "And I don't want to tell on the kids at school."

Ashley thought for a moment. "Well, why don't they just tell the teacher they were cheating by accident?"

Keisha tried not to smile. "Oh, Ash, this is different. They can't do that."

"Why not? Mama says you won't get in trouble if you tell the truth."

Before Keisha could come up with an explanation she thought her sister would understand, the door swung open and Mr. Vance walked in. Keisha breathed a sigh of relief.

"*Daddy!*" cried the two younger children, running to wrap their arms around their father's legs.

"How are my little brown bears? Did you have a good day? Did you mind your big sister?"

"Yes, Daddy." Ronnie looked very solemn. "I *prombised* Kee-kee I wouldn't go into your *vegable* garden, and I stayed way far away."

"We were *very* good," said Ashley, as Mr. Vance rubbed Ronnie's curly brown hair. "But some of Keisha's friends at school weren't so good, and—"

"Ashley!" exclaimed Keisha, jumping up from the table. She thought fast. She wasn't ready to talk to her parents about any of this. "Daddy, don't pay attention to her. It was just a story my friends and I were discussing."

Benjamin Vance set his briefcase on the counter and swung Ronnie and Ashley up into his arms. He walked over to Keisha and, balancing Ronnie in the crook of his elbow, gave her shoulder a squeeze. "Listen, Keisha-girl, I'm too tired to cook. I picked up some barbecued chicken. So why don't you get those French fries out of the freezer and microwave them for a few minutes. When you've finished with the salad and set the table, we'll eat. And I'll do the dishes afterward, okay?"

"It's a deal," said Keisha, giving him a big smile. "Dad, do you mind if I go over to Ellie's after supper?

I promise I won't stay long."

"Fine with me, honey. Just be back by eight-thirty." Mr. Vance added, with a big wink, "It's a school night, in case you've forgotten."

Keisha tried to keep her voice cheery. "How could I forget?"

She turned back to the salad as her father and Ronnie disappeared into the den and Ashley ran to fetch a picture she'd drawn in school that morning. By the time everyone was seated around the table, Keisha realized that she wasn't hungry. She took charge of helping Ronnie, whose skills with eating utensils were still shaky, and occasionally pushed her own food around on her plate. The minute everyone had finished, she jumped up, mumbled a quick good-bye, grabbed her jacket, and hurried out the door.

Keisha was glad to be outside. The fresh air and the walking helped clear her mind. The whole situation was so complicated, and Ashley had really gotten to her with her questions. She looked forward to sitting in one of Ellie's overstuffed chairs and relaxing awhile. She might even talk it over with Ellie. Or maybe she'd just go up to the attic.

Keisha walked up the steps to Ellie's front door and lifted the heavy brass knocker. The big Victorian house was the prettiest on the block. Everyone seemed to know Ellie, and she was always busy with her music students and all of her projects. It made Keisha feel extra special to know that she and her friends could visit Ellie's whenever they wanted to.

The wide wooden door opened. "Hello, Keisha dear. Come right in." Ellie hung Keisha's jacket and ushered her into the sitting room. She settled into her big, comfortable armchair, and Keisha took a seat near her. "I was just beginning a new book by one of my favorite authors," said Ellie, peering over her reading glasses. "But tell me, how was your day, Keisha?"

The words spilled out. "Oh, Ellie, something happened at school today and I just don't know what to do!" She told Ellie everything.

"I know you'll make the right decision," Ellie said when Keisha had finished talking.

Keisha wished she felt as confident about that as Ellie sounded. Her mouth puckered as she sat silently picking at a loose thread on her shirt. Finally, she looked up

again. "You know, I was thinking about going up to the attic for a little while. I need a break from thinking about all of this."

"That's an excellent idea. I'll be right here if you need me, dear."

Lost in thought, Keisha took the golden key from the entry hall and slowly made her way to the second floor. She fit the key into the lock, turned the brass knob, and gave the door a little push. At the head of the attic stairs, she stopped. Everything seemed familiar and friendly, from the old dressmaker's form in one corner to the stack of luggage in another.

Still moving slowly, Keisha walked over to the huge steamer trunk and lifted the heavy lid. She couldn't believe her eyes. Right on top was a long, white satin gown with a fur collar. The outer layer of iridescent mesh matched the sparkling crown that rested in the folds of fabric. Beside the crown was a pair of white leather boots topped with soft white fur.

Keisha immediately slipped into the outfit. She held the crown steady on her head and dashed over to the mirror. She looked just like a fairy queen! Rubbing the glorious white fabric on her arms, she gazed at her reflection with a smile.

Then her smile disappeared.

Chapter

Three

WELCOME, QUEEN KEISHA

Keisha's mouth fell open and her eyes grew wide as she looked around her. The wind blew graceful snowdrifts against the surrounding hills, constantly changing the shape of the land. Evergreen branches heavy with ice refracted the light into a bright rainbow of colors against the sky. The crystaline wonderland sparkled like the diamond and emerald and amethyst birthstones that Keisha and her friends talked about getting for their birthdays.

Where am I, Keisha wondered. What is this strange and beautiful place?

It took a few moments even to realize that she was in a silvery sleigh drawn by two violet ponies with shimmering manes. A golden-haired girl was sitting at her side. Keisha couldn't help staring. The girl's skin was pale purple! Keisha rubbed her eyes.

The girl smiled and shifted the reins in her hands. "I'm sorry I woke you, your Majesty," she said. "All this ice has made the road very rough."

Keisha looked blankly at her. There was no one else around, so the girl *must* have been speaking to her!

"Who are you?" she finally asked.

The girl's laugh rang out. "Why, I am Mela, of course. That must have been quite a nap!"

Keisha smiled, then shivered—her lovely gown gave her little protection from the cold breeze—and yawned. It was easy to play along with Mela's impression that she'd been asleep. Even in her dreams, she had never seen such a strange and spectacular place.

Mela halted the ponies. "The cold will soon clear your Majesty's head." She placed a

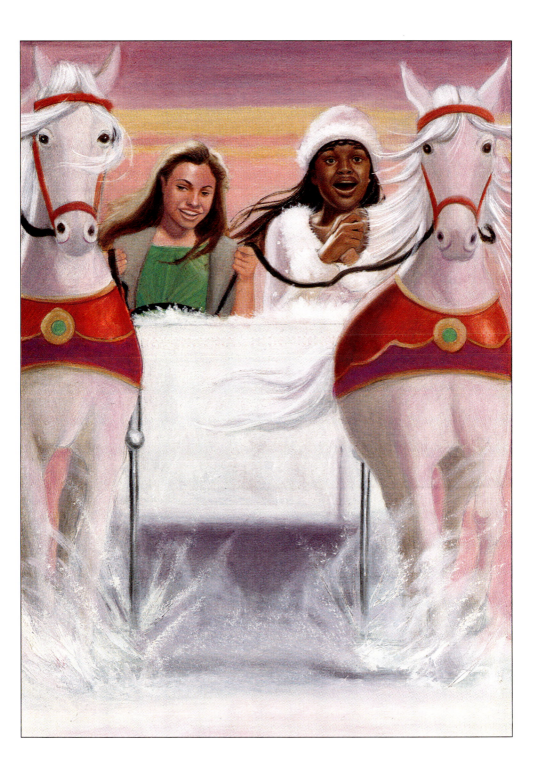

white fur hat in Keisha's lap and reached over to tuck a thick, furry blanket over her legs.

"Thank you, Mela," said Keisha, removing her crown and pulling on the warm hat.

"I shall keep the crown safe for my Queen," said Mela. "We are not far from the palace now." She snapped the reins and pulled her shawl closer about her shoulders. Keisha asked the girl to tell her about herself.

Mela smiled shyly. "I am still in school. I hope to work in my father's field someday." Then her eyes clouded and her smile disappeared.

"What does your father do?" asked Keisha.

"He is a quarrier, mining the shining crystals. Or he did. Now he is too ill to work. My brother, Antal, held a favored post in the palace, but now he cares for Father at home." Mela frowned. "We live there, on Mount Aurora." She pointed to a high mountain that sparkled in the distance as if it were made of a million chips of antique glass.

"It seems so incredibly bright!" exclaimed Keisha.

"Oh, your Majesty, have you forgotten so quickly how it used to be?" Mela looked even sadder. "Not long ago, it shone almost like the sun itself."

The girls fell silent for a time, and the sleigh sped over the icy ground.

"It's all so beautiful," Keisha said with a sigh, though her nose was tingling.

"There is no place more beautiful than the Crystal Kingdom," Mela said quietly. "Even now."

Before Keisha could ask what she meant, Mela pointed to a dark shape down the road. As they drew near, Keisha saw that it was a small child. Keisha jumped down and scooped the crying boy up in her arms. Except for his pale purple face and hands, he reminded her of Ronnie when he got frightened or hurt. "What's the matter?" she asked.

"My brother and sister are having a—an argument!" cried the little boy.

"Oh, is that all? That's nothing to worry about," said Keisha. She didn't see why he was so upset. It usually took Ronnie and Ashley only a few minutes to get over their quarrels.

Mela gave Keisha a puzzled look, then turned to the child. "Where do you live, little one?" she asked.

Shivering silently in Keisha's arms, the boy pointed to a group of houses down the road.

"Poor little fellow," she whispered. "We must get him

home, Mela." Keisha seated the boy in the sleigh and wrapped the blanket tightly around him. Then she clambered in, hugging her chest for warmth as Mela urged the ponies forward.

What's happening here? wondered Keisha when they reached the village. Several bonfires threw orange reflections over the snow. People of all ages—all of them purple, like Mela and the boy—huddled as near the flames as they could. A number of the men and women shouted to Mela to stop.

The girls stepped out of the sleigh, and the villagers gathered around them. "Your Majesty, help us," cried a pale orchid-skinned woman wrapped in a fuschia cloak. "My little ones are nearly frozen." She pointed to  three shivering youngsters crouched at her feet. "You must do something. Please."

Keisha turned to her companion. "Is it this way everywhere?"

Mela nodded sadly. "It became very cold while you were away. Everything seems to be changing."

Some of the villagers began to argue about what might be causing the kingdom's troubles. A scuffle broke out at the edge of the crowd.

Mela became anxious. "We must get to the palace, my Queen," she said, tugging at Keisha's sleeve.

When Keisha had found the little boy's family and placed him safely in his father's arms, she promised the villagers that she would do everything in her power to help them. She and Mela climbed back into the sleigh.

Mela frowned as she turned the ponies toward the palace. "Something is terribly wrong." She seemed almost to be speaking to herself. "I have heard of disputes and anger elsewhere, but until now, harsh words were unknown in the Crystal Kingdom. We have always lived in peace and harmony. Now everyone is quarrelsome and uneasy . . . and afraid . . ." Her voice trailed off.

The only sounds were those of the sleigh's runners shushing over the snow and the ponies' muffled hoofbeats as they flew across the sparkling landscape. In her mind, Keisha still heard the crying of the frightened little boy she had held in her arms. She pulled the snow-white blanket closer about her.

She was the Queen of the Crystal Kingdom now. How could she keep her promise to help her people?

NO OTHER CHOICE

Mela handed Keisha the crown and took back the hat as the sleigh passed through a high crystal archway and into a wide courtyard. A breathtaking crystal structure rose before Keisha, blocking out the sky. Graceful pillars and columns framed windows as big as Keisha's bedroom wall. Her eyes followed the glinting columns up and up and up.

Suddenly, a frantic little man with long gray hair came rushing up to the sleigh. He extended a pale purple hand to Keisha, gesturing wildly that she was to climb down. His soft velvet robe, a deep violet covered with gold and silver stars, shimmered in the sun. The stars on his tall pointed hat glinted when he reached up to steady it.

"Queen Keisha! Queen Keisha!" the man cried, bowing low. "Please, you must come at once!"

"What is it?" asked Keisha.

The man seemed to notice Mela for the first time. "Take care of the horses, Mela. I shall send for you if you are needed."

"Of course, Sage," Mela replied. Before Keisha could even thank the girl for bringing her to the palace, the man was pulling her toward the doorway.

"Forgive my rudeness, your Majesty, but the Council of Elders awaits on a *most* urgent matter."

The Sage led her into a huge chamber made entirely of crystal. Keisha's mouth opened wide in amazement. Columns of glass, some delicately carved and others rough-hewn, appeared to grow right out of the floor and even the walls. Beams of light shot across the chamber and bounced off the floor, flashing all the colors of the rainbow.

He glanced around, then cupped his hands to his mouth as he whispered to Keisha: "The Energy Crystal is missing from the Arc of Fire, your Majesty. I made the terrible discovery some days ago. I did not want to alarm anyone, so at first I searched alone for it. Then I told the council so that they could help. But we have found nothing, not even the silver basket that held the Crystal." He paused to catch his breath. "We are in terrible danger!"

The Sage led Keisha through a portal and into a long hallway. The walls slanted outward in a giant "V" shape. The crystal was translucent: it let light in everywhere, but she couldn't see clearly through it. Keisha nearly forgot the anxious little man at her side until he cleared his throat to speak again.

Keisha couldn't think of anything to say that wouldn't give her away, but her silence didn't seem to matter. The Sage continued whispering as he rushed her along the hallway. "Only the Sages know the secret of the Energy Crystal. Now that the Crystal is missing, I must reveal everything to you, my Queen." He glanced all around before continuing. "It is the Crystal that gives our kingdom its warmth and its famed brilliant color. It is the source of harmony and tranquility and keeps our kingdom in order. For age upon age, ever since it was carried down from the peak of Mount Aurora, the Sages have been its guardians. With the help of the young people of the land, we tend the Energy Crystal and maintain the Arc of Fire."

The Sage stopped and looked deep into Keisha's eyes. "Nothing has ever been stolen in our kingdom before. Since the Crystal disappeared, our world has steadily grown colder and weaker. Our peace has been lost. Why, this morning several fistfights were even reported. The ice has begun to take over, and . . . ."

"Yes?" said Keisha. "Go ahead, tell me all."

"Your Majesty, if the Crystal is not returned to the Arc of Fire, the entire Crystal Kingdom will turn to ice. We have very little time, perhaps only another day. After that, we will be frozen in time—forever!"

Keisha gasped. Before she could say another word, the Sage opened a pair of huge double doors, bowed, and pointed into the room beyond. "The council awaits you, your Majesty."

She straightened her back and raised her chin as she entered an enormous room. Six small men and women sat in carved crystal chairs around a long table. One of them arose and pulled out the largest crystal chair at the head of the table for her.

Keisha's mind was racing as she sat down. She cleared

her throat. "Council of Elders," she began solemnly. "You know that the Energy Crystal is missing. The Sage has just given me even graver news: the Crystal Kingdom is in great danger. Without the Crystal, life as we know it will cease to exist!" The elders looked at one another in shocked silence. "You can see the changes already, warmth and color and energy are being drained away. We *must* find the Crystal."

The elders immediately began to debate and argue just like the villagers over what was to be done. Keisha's heart sank, and for a moment she was tempted to run out the door. What *should* she do now?

"Elders!" she shouted. The council fell silent. "Our people depend on us to keep the kingdom as peaceful and happy as it has always been. But that will not happen unless we find the Crystal and the person who is responsible for taking it."

"But, my Queen, we have so little time," protested the Sage, "and I have already searched the palace. In just a day or so we may be too weak to do anything. How will we find the culprit before it is too late?"

Keisha tried to sound strong. "We must tell our people the secret of the Crystal, Sage, and get them to help us find it."

The elders groaned, and the oldest one rose to his feet. "We cannot do that, your Majesty," he said. "If the people find out the Energy Crystal is missing, everyone will panic."

"We have no other choice," Keisha said with conviction. "We must tell the truth and get everyone to work together." She looked into each of the elders' eyes. "I want you to send word to the people that their queen wishes to speak with them immediately."

The elders exchanged glances. "As you wish, your Majesty," said the Sage. To Keisha's pleasant surprise, he bowed his head to her and the other council members did likewise.

The Sage escorted Keisha to the palace entrance, and the council members followed. When Keisha stepped onto the balcony, a large throng had already gathered. The seven councilors solemnly arranged themselves behind her as the crowd moved in closer to hear their queen. Keisha looked out over the sea of lavender and orchid and fuschia shimmering before her. Hundreds of small, pale purple faces turned to her. A cold wind blew at her gown and whisked her long brown hair about.

Keisha shivered, and a chill ran up her spine. What if I'm wrong? What if everyone *does* panic? But how can the elders and I find the Crystal alone? Keisha cleared her throat and spoke as loudly as she could.

"Thank you, kind citizens, for coming here today. You all know that things are not right in the Crystal Kingdom. It is because the Energy Crystal is missing—"

"Missing!" cried a dozen voices. Keisha could just make out some of the comments of the nearest citizens: "How can it be missing? Nothing has ever disappeared from here before." "Is this why the kingdom is turning cold?" "What will happen to us?"

Keisha raised her hands for silence. "We must find the Crystal together and return it to its proper place at once."

"The Crystal may be important to *you*, your Majesty," called one woman. "But all that matters to *me* is keeping my family from freezing."

"I don't see how we can help," shouted a man. "We came here to find out how you could help *us*!"

Keisha's confidence wavered, but she reminded herself to be strong. "I will do all I can, of course. But we are *all* citizens of the kingdom and this problem affects every one of us, so you must do your part as well. Someone must have the courage to tell us what has happened. I am certain that when we find the Crystal, everything will return to normal. Go now. We have very little time."

Then Keisha turned to the Sage. "Order my sleigh, please. I, too, will search for the Energy Crystal. If need be, I will travel to the peak of Mount Aurora myself to try and find another one."

The Sage's eyes were wide as he accompanied her into the palace. "Your Majesty!" he cried. "That is a dangerous journey even in the best of times. The paths are steep and narrow, and the gorges are hundreds of feet deep. Now there are rumors that avalanches have blocked many of the passes, and . . ."

Keisha's reply was firm. "My mind is made up. Mela knows the way. She will be my guide."

"If you insist, my Queen," said the Sage. "But I have something to give you for the journey."

Chapter

Five

A
TREACHEROUS
JOURNEY

The Sage led Keisha to an alcove. Taking a small silver key from his pocket, he opened a massive crystal cabinet. Ever so carefully, he lifted out an iridescent wand. At its tip, an exquisite crystal snowflake sparkled softly.

"It is beautiful," Keisha sighed. The wand seemed to have a special way of capturing light.

"The royal wand has certain powers," the Sage explained, "powers to keep the person holding it safe,

powers to fulfill pure wishes. I took it for safekeeping when I found that the Energy Crystal was missing." He shook his head sadly as he looked at the lovely wand. "It has faded, too, like all else in the Crystal Kingdom. Still, it might be of some use to your Majesty. It may have power to fulfill one more wish." Solemnly, the Sage handed the wand to Keisha. "You must go quickly."

In the courtyard, the Sage steadied the violet ponies while Keisha and Mela climbed into the sleigh and Keisha again placed the white fur hat over her dark hair. Then he spread the thick furry blanket across their laps and tucked it around them. The Sage looked very tired and cold, and he seemed paler than when Keisha had first seen him. She smiled to reassure him.

"I am grateful for your concern, Sage. I am in good hands with Mela, and we will be careful travelers."

"May good fortune be yours, your Majesty," the Sage said. "And ours," he added in a whisper. Then he tapped the nearest pony on the rump and they pranced away, their manes and tails flying and their hooves ringing on the icy roadway.

Soon there were no houses in sight. Keisha snuggled into the blanket, again enchanted by the countryside that flew past the speeding sleigh. For the time being, at least, the kingdom still looked like a perfect wonderland. In the quiet moments that passed, she thought of what it must have been like, this peaceable kingdom where harmony prevailed. She could not let it be lost forever.

After a while, the once vibrant ponies seemed to slow down. Keisha wondered whether their energy was already fading. Mela appeared to be lost in deep thoughts of her own.

"How much farther?" Keisha asked as they entered a small village. The people looked much like those who had crowded the palace gate.

"The distance is less than on our route to the palace," said Mela. "Ahead you can see Mount Aurora, which is my home." She sighed as she looked at the villagers. "These children are so pale. They sit like blocks of stone, too tired for ice tag or a good snowball game. Still, it is good that we will stop here. Our young ponies are growing as weary as old nags."

When Keisha told the villagers of the emergency, they said they knew nothing of the whereabouts of the Energy Crystal. They shivered beneath their heavy coats, rubbing their hands and stamping their feet to try to warm them. Disputes soon broke out over who had more fuel to keep warm and who might be responsible for their troubles.

"Please," said Keisha, "do not let your fear lead you into hurtful quarrels. This problem affects our entire kingdom, and together we will find the solution to our troubles. But I can do nothing without your help. You must report any news of the Crystal immediately. And just as important, you must take care of one another. Help your friends and neighbors to survive the cold as best you can."

Keisha could see that her words made some difference. The villagers seemed embarrassed over behaving badly in the presence of their queen, and calm discussions began about who would search what areas. They nodded as they waved good-bye to Keisha.

The ponies trotted on with renewed energy, kicking up small eddies of snow. But their pace soon slowed again, even though the ground was fairly level. The air grew colder. The girls' hair was coated with frost, and their breath formed dense clouds in the air. They soon stopped talking as their words slipped away on the wind and they shivered beneath the furry, white blanket. Keisha's spirits began to fall as fast as the temperature.

At the foot of Mount Aurora, the path grew more difficult, just as the Sage had warned. Keisha tried not to worry, but it was hard to tell the perilous ice from the roadway. She only hoped that Mela could see the difference.

The exhausted ponies struggled to pull the sleigh uphill, often sliding backward on the slippery surface.

The path narrowed to little more than a small ledge. On one side, the mountain rose tall and steep toward the sky. On the other, it fell away sharply into a deep gorge. Keisha squeezed her eyes shut as they rounded a hairpin turn.

Suddenly a cracking, splintering sound echoed off the mountainsides. The ponies whinnied loudly, and one let out a fearful scream. Mela and Keisha slid from the sleigh to the ground, shaken but unhurt. One of the ponies had fallen, and its leg was wedged in a deep crevasse.

Mela unfastened the harness and led the uninjured pony a safe distance down the path, then hurried back. "If I hold the pony, your Majesty, perhaps you might try to free his hoof . . ." Mela began talking softly to the frightened animal as she gently stroked his forehead.

Keisha knelt and ran her hand down the pony's trapped leg, feeling for his hoof below the icy surface. It did not budge when she tried to pull it out.

Mela handed Keisha a shard of crystal. "Here, try this."

Using the shard like a pick, Keisha began to chip at the ice. It was slow, hard work. Small beads of perspiration tickled beneath her warm fur hat. Little by little, the hole became bigger. When the pony finally broke free, Keisha nearly lost her balance. Mela cheered happily as he backed away from the crevasse.

The girls led the limping animal to a wider section of the path to inspect his injured leg. It bled from a cut just above the hoof, but the leg wasn't broken.

"The bleeding will stop soon," Mela assured Keisha. "I think he was more frightened than injured. But it would be unwise to try to go on with him. We must leave him here and fetch him later."

From the sleigh, Mela brought two lengths of rope and a woolen rug. While Keisha secured the rug over the injured pony's back and tied him to a tree, Mela adjusted the traces for the one pony who would take them onward.

Chapter Six

THE
TRUTH!

The little search party crossed the break in the ice and continued upward. The brave pony climbed slowly, slipping again and again. The jagged boulders and the few scraggly trees that clung to the mountainside were black against the darkening sky. Keisha was shivering. It was twilight already—so little time was left!

"Your Majesty, I . . ." Mela began. Her voice trembled, and she shook her head. "Is this all because of the Energy Crystal? Could it possibly be that something else is

causing the cold and fading and exhaustion?" Mela
rubbed her pale lavender palms together.

"I don't want to frighten you, Mela," said Keisha, "but
the Energy Crystal is more powerful than anyone realizes.
That is why we must find it. Perhaps I shouldn't admit
this, but I am also frightened. We all have to be strong."

Mela fell silent and urged the pony onward. To Keisha,
the narrow road appeared impossibly steep.

In the distance, Keisha saw a house on the snow-
covered plateau, lit by the rising moon and nestled
among a grove of tall trees. Warm light spilled from the
windows out onto the darkly gleaming snow. Beyond the
house, the pathway continued to rise steeply up Mount
Aurora.

"That house looks so warm," commented Keisha,
pointing towards the grove.

Mela sighed. "It is my home."

"Oh, Mela, do you think we could stop there for a few
minutes?" Keisha's hands and feet ached with cold, and
she could see that Mela was terribly tired.

"My father is very ill!" cried Mela. "I do not think that
would be a good idea. Besides, we must go on. You have
said we have so little time."

"Don't you want to stop and see him?" Keisha asked.

Just then the sleigh lurched and began to slide

backward. The pony had lost his footing completely!

The girls quickly climbed down and put all their weight behind the sleigh, pushing hard and trying to keep their feet from slipping. Finally the pony's hooves rang against a clear stretch of pathway and he managed to jerk the sleigh forward. Mela hurried to grab the reins, guided him to a wide and level spot, and unharnessed him.

"What are you doing?" Keisha asked.

"I'm sorry, your Majesty, but we will have to walk from here." Mela was panting, and her breath formed small clouds in the air. "The path will grow even steeper, and now it is much too slippery for the pony. He can't possibly pull the sleigh any farther."

Keisha's legs felt weak as she slipped the wand inside her boot and followed behind Mela. The path was so slick that they slid more than walked. Sometimes it was easier to crawl. They grabbed at frozen chunks of ice, branches, and crystals to pull themselves forward, hoping these handholds wouldn't snap off as they clambered on.

"Mela, we have to stop soon," Keisha whispered. She couldn't tell whether it was because of the extreme chill or the thin mountain air, but her whole chest ached every time she inhaled.

Finally the path became a little less steep, and eventually it was almost level again. The girls were just able to walk upright. Keisha wanted to shout for joy, but she couldn't seem to get any air. Her hands and feet burned painfully from the cold, and her hair was covered with frost.

"We can rest now, your Majesty." Mela was gasping for breath, too. Both girls collapsed on the snow. "Your Majesty, what will happen if we don't find the Crystal?" she asked after a few minutes.

Keisha chose her words carefully. "Well, life in the Crystal Kingdom will not be as we know it now. The whole kingdom depends on the Energy Crystal, and we must find the person who knows its whereabouts." She glanced toward the high peak of Mount Aurora. Keisha's eyes filled with tears. "But I don't think I can make it to the top and back in time."

Mela began to sob. "This is all my fault!"

"Mela, what are you talking about?"

"It was . . . my brother and I who took the Crystal!"

Keisha was stunned. "What do you mean? Why would you do that?" she asked softly.

"For our father. He has been out of his head with pain and fever, your Majesty, and nothing we tried has done him any good." Mela continued haltingly. "My brother Antal is one of the young people who helped to maintain the Energy Crystal in the Arc."

"Go on," said Keisha.

"Everyone knows the Energy Crystal has special powers, especially the people who tend it. So when our father became so terribly ill, Antal came up with a plan to save him. He discussed it with me. We agreed that he would borrow the Crystal and take it home . . ."

"Why hasn't one of you said something? The entire kingdom is at risk."

"Antal doesn't know all that has happened." Mela wiped tears from her face. "We meant no harm."

"But *you* know the danger. You should have spoken sooner when you saw what was happening," she gently reminded her.

"I was afraid of what might happen to Antal and me. No one in the kingdom has ever done anything truly bad, and I—I was afraid we would be exiled. I cannot imagine having to live anywhere else. Besides, Antal is convinced that the Crystal will help Father if it is near him. But now I've botched everything. Please, isn't there some way we can just return the Crystal and say we found it lying by the side of the road? No one would have to know . . . I don't want us to be banished!"

"Mela, that is not the way. You must believe me. Now hurry! We may still have time to save the kingdom. Lead me to your home."

As the girls stumbled wearily toward the house, someone came running out, shouting. Mela looked at Keisha and smiled for the first time in hours.

"It is my brother, Antal!" she cried.

Chapter

Seven

THE
RETURN
HOME

A crackling fire blazed on the hearth. Antal watched the girls from the doorway while they warmed themselves. When Keisha looked around, she saw a man lying on a small cot near the fireplace. She gasped. He was so pale! His eyes were closed and he hardly moved.

She took the wand from her boot and sat down beside him. Keisha gazed at the thin crystal wand. Hadn't the Sage said that the wand would keep her and those around her safe? And hadn't he said that it might have one wish left? It was certainly worth a chance.

"Oh, please make him well," Keisha whispered, holding the wand above the sick man. "He simply must get better." Slowly, carefully, she passed the wand over his body and touched it to his forehead. Keisha closed her eyes. "Please," she whispered again.

Mela and Antal watched from a corner, then went over to the bed.

Antal bowed solemnly. "Your Majesty, my sister has explained everything. I didn't know what would happen when I took the Crystal, and staying here to watch over Father, I had no idea of the—" He fell silent for a moment. "It is all my fault. Mela only—"

Keisha interrupted him. "We have no time to lose. Go quickly and get the Crystal. We will also need rope and anything that will help us travel speedily." Antal seemed hesitant. "Is something wrong?" she asked.

"My father . . ."

"Antal, the Energy Crystal has great powers, but it cannot heal your father alone. I have done all that I can for him . . ." She glanced at the bed, then continued. "You know the Crystal is not for your family but for the entire kingdom. Please."

Without another word, Antal
reached under his father's pillow.
When he pulled out his hand, it
held the Energy Crystal—a
multifaceted wonder of a jewel
that glowed dimly in the light
from the fire. Then Antal fetched its
silver basket with the soft cushion inside and placed
everything in Keisha's lap.

Antal cleared his throat. "Your Majesty, I am ready
to do what I must."

Keisha looked again at the ailing man. Something
about him had changed. Could it be true? His eyes
appeared to be moving under his closed lids. His chest
rose and fell more strongly with each breath.

"Father!" exclaimed Mela and Antal. They knelt at
the bed and took the man's pale hands in theirs, then
looked up at Keisha. "Thank you, your Majesty," Antal
whispered.

Mela's eyes were troubled, though, and her mouth
formed a frown. "Oh, your Majesty," she cried, "I am so
sorry for what we did!"

Keisha placed her hands on Mela's shoulders. "Mela,
our countrymen are the ones who deserve an apology,
not I. I am glad your father seems better. Please stay

here and care for him. Antal must return with me and explain what you and he have done."

Mela began to cry.

"Don't worry," Keisha said to comfort her. "I know the elders will be fair."

Mela prepared warm drinks while Antal gathered supplies. He carefully set the Crystal and its delicate silver basket in his pack. Keisha sipped the steaming broth that Mela handed to her. It warmed her right down to her toes. Then they were ready to depart.

At the door, Mela cried, "Wait!" She put her hand to her neck. "I hope you will accept this small sign of our thanks for everything you have done for us. It belonged to our mother." She placed a delicate heart-shaped silver pendant in Keisha's palm.

Keisha pulled the girl close and kissed her cheek, then stepped out into the dark, windy night.

"We will send back word as soon as we can," Keisha called as she and Antal began to trudge through the cold.

The temperature had dropped even further, and mounds of snow that earlier had felt soft underfoot were now solid and sheathed in ice. Keisha shivered and pulled her fur-lined hat down over her ears.

Although they had picks, ropes, and walking sticks to help them keep their balance, they still slid and fell on the steep, icy slope. Keisha's nose felt numb, and her fingers tingled painfully with the cold. The moonlight turned the rocks and bumps into long, strange shadows on the roadway.

When they came upon the sleigh, Keisha wondered aloud whether they might chance using it, but Antal said it would be too dangerous. He gave the pony some food from his pack and placed a blanket over its back. Then Keisha and Antal slipped and slithered on down the mountain.

"There's the other pony!" Keisha cried at last.

Antal fed him, too, and checked his bandage. "It will do until I return," he said.

Just when Keisha began to wonder whether they would freeze in their tracks, the sight of a village ahead gave them hope. She and Antal knocked at the first house they came to. A shivering, sleepy man answered. "My Queen!" he gasped. Without question, he helped to saddle two horses and wished them well.

Keisha and Antal rode as swiftly as they dared, stopping to rest the horses only when the palace walls came into view. Keisha gazed thoughtfully at her weary companion. "Antal, do you know what you must do now?"

"Yes, your Majesty." Antal's voice trembled, and his head was bowed. "The moment the Crystal is in place, I will go before the elders and tell them what happened. I have put peoples' lives at risk, and I will accept whatever punishment is decreed."

"Yes, that is what you must do," Keisha said softly, "and if we are not too late, the kingdom will be safe now."

The journey had taken just under a day, but Keisha was shocked at the change. Everything in the Crystal City had faded incredibly. The few people she saw were motionless, huddled in pale, trembling groups around whatever heat they could find. Perhaps she had arrived too late to do any good.

Antal led Keisha to the Arc of Fire. She took the Energy Crystal from its basket, ascended the steps to the Arc, and placed the Crystal on its high, narrow pedestal.

With Antal at her side, Keisha then went to look for the Sage. It was time for him to speak to the elders. When she found the Sage, he was exhausted and nearly colorless. He shivered violently as she briefly explained the situation.

Antal knew he must face the Council of Elders alone. His shoulders slumped and he dug his hands into his pockets as the Sage slowly led him toward the chamber.

An hour later, the Sage led Antal back into the hall where Keisha waited. She felt as if she had been holding her breath the whole time. But the elders must have dealt fairly with Antal. His eyes shone with relief and he returned her smile.

They all waited together in silence while the sun crawled to its midpoint in the sky. Keisha walked around the palace. Color was slowly returning to the palace guards and she could feel the chill leaving the air. The bells tolled the noon hour at last, and Keisha knew the kingdom was safe.

Keisha sent word that the citizens should be called to the palace once more. When she announced that the Energy Crystal had been returned and the danger had passed, the cheering shook the ground. People stomped and clapped and danced in circles. Groups of children started noisy games of ice tag.

Soon everything will be back to normal, thought Keisha. My time here is finished. She thanked the people, the elders, and the Sage for all they had done.

"My Queen, *you* have done it all!" cried the Sage, a new energy filling the little man with joy.

Then Keisha turned and disappeared into the palace. She whispered good-bye to the Crystal Kingdom as she reentered the mirrored hall—and Ellie Goodwin's attic.

Chapter
Eight

A MAJESTIC
SOLUTION

Keisha quickly slipped out
of the dress and crown and
boots. She carefully laid the outfit
in the trunk and closed the lid.

With a last glance around the attic, Keisha pulled the
cord to turn off the light, ran down the steps, and shut
the door behind her. When she heard the lock click, she
bounded down to the sitting room. Ellie looked up from
her book as Keisha rushed into the room.

"Ellie, I had the most magnificent adventure yet! I can hardly believe it all happened!"

Ellie's warm, friendly smile lit up her face. "I'm so pleased for you, my dear. You must tell me about it some other time, though. Your father called and asked me to remind you that it's a school night."

"Thanks, Ellie," Keisha replied, fastening her jacket. "I'd better get home then."

Ellie walked Keisha to the door, turned on the porch light, and wished her goodnight. Keisha blew her a kiss as she ran down the walkway.

Keisha must have fallen asleep even before she'd turned off the light. The next thing she knew, someone was tucking a blanket around her shoulders. It was so nice to be really warm.

"Thank you, Sage," she murmured.

"Who's Sage?" asked a very familiar voice.

"Mama? How did you get here?"

Mrs. Vance smiled. "I live here, remember?"

"I think I was having a dream." Keisha snuggled deeper under the downy blanket.

"Sweet dreams, baby. I'll see you tomorrow."

"Night, Mama."

Keisha was the first to arrive at the table she shared

with her friends at lunchtime. Alison got to the point the minute she sat down: "So, what did you decide?"

"Well, the first thing I decided to do was visit the attic."

"That's exactly what I would have done," exclaimed Heather.

When Keisha described the Crystal Kingdom, the girls could hardly contain their amazement.

"I wish I could have seen the ponies," said Megan, with a dreamy look in her eyes.

"As soon as I have my chores done this afternoon,"

said Heather, "I'm going to get my paints and mix as many shades of purple as I can. Imagine a whole *kingdom* of purples!"

The girls ate slowly while Keisha told them about saving her Crystal Kingdom.

"*Your* kingdom?" Alison asked, giving Megan a wink.

"It really felt like my kingdom. Everything was so real that I almost forgot about coming home. I wish you all could have been there."

Heather joined in the teasing. "So you decided the solution to the problem with Deanna is to act like a queen from now on?"

"I think Keisha has always been very regal." Megan's mischievous green eyes twinkled.

"Oh, come on, you guys," Keisha said with a laugh. "What I mean is, it helped me see a lot of things." The girls talked a while longer, then threw away their trash and went out to play tetherball.

When the final bell rang, Keisha told her friends she would talk to them later. She mustered her courage and followed Deanna into the noisy hallway. "Deanna, wait. Could we talk for a minute?"

Deanna stopped. "I guess so. What's up?"

"Remember the math test yesterday?"

"How could I forget? It was so hard!"

I guess I have to just come right out with it, thought Keisha. "You and William were cheating, weren't you?" she said quietly.

Deanna gave her a long, hard look, but her cheeks turned red as she spoke. "Cheating! What makes you think that? I almost always get top grades on tests."

Keisha hesitated again, then plunged on. "Deanna, you *know* I saw you writing on the test paper after you read William's note . . ." She glanced at Deanna's pouting face. "Look, I don't really care what grades you get in school, and at first I wasn't sure what I should do. But the rest of us work hard to do well and earn our grades fair and square. It's just not fair for you to get a good grade without working for it, too."

Deanna scuffed her toes on the floor, then sighed. "I usually study hard, but this time I just didn't. I was getting panicky, and I was cramming by the lockers before school started. William saw me and asked what was up. He offered to give me some of the answers. My whole family's so good at math, I'm not sure my folks would understand if I messed up on a test." She took a big breath. "You didn't tell on me, did you?"

"No," said Keisha, shaking her head. "But one of us has to tell Ms. Joseph. Otherwise it's as if you stole your test score from the rest of us."

The girls stood looking at each other for a minute. Finally, Deanna turned and slowly headed for the classroom where Ms. Joseph usually planned her lessons for the following day.

Keisha walked down the hall to her locker.

Diary

Dear Diary,

I still can't believe I was the Queen of the Crystal Kingdom. It was a little scary at times. I don't mean just getting up the mountain, but being responsible for so many people. That's a lot harder than just taking care of two little kids like Ronnie and Ashley a few hours a day. It's not always so easy to figure out what's good for everybody. I'm glad everything turned out okay!

Everything turned out okay at school, too. It was hard to talk to Deanna about her cheating on the test. But Ellie was right—I made the best decision. I stood up for what I believe and got Deanna to do what's fair for the whole class.

In the morning, my mom said I'd been talking about somebody named Sage in my sleep, and she asked whether I remembered my dream. I only told her the part about being a Queen. I hope I don't talk in my sleep very often.

It would sure be cool if I could take my camera on an adventure. I could bring back pictures so the Magic Attic Club could see the Sage and Mela and the palace. It was incredible!

Sweet dreams, Diary

Keisha

P.S. When Deanna told Ms. Joseph that she cheated, Ms. Joseph was real understanding. Plus, she's letting Deanna and William take a make-up test! I think that's more than fair.

JOIN THE MAGIC ATTIC CLUB!

You can enjoy every adventure of the Magic Attic Club just by reading all the books. And there's more!

You can have a whole world of fun with the dolls, outfits, and accessories that are based on the books. And since Alison, Keisha, Heather, and Megan can wear one another's clothes, you can relive their adventures, or create new ones of your own!

To join the Magic Attic Club, just fill out this postcard and drop it in the mail, or call toll free **1-800-221-6972**. We'll send you a **free** membership kit

including a poster, bookmark, postcards, and a catalog with all four dolls.

With your first purchase of a doll, you'll also receive your own key to the attic. And it's FREE!

Yes, I want to join the Magic Attic Club!

My name is _____

My address is _____

City _____ State _____ Zip _____

Birth date _____ Parent's Signature _____

11915

And send a catalog to my friend, too!

My friend's name is _____

Address _____

City _____ State _____ Zip _____

11916

If someone has already used the postcard from
this book and you would like a free Magic Attic Club
catalog, just send your full name and address to:

Magic Attic Club
866 Spring Street
P.O. Box 9712
Portland, ME 04104-9954

Or call toll free
1-800-775-9272

Code: 11917

BUSINESS REPLY MAIL

FIRST-CLASS MAIL PERMIT NO. 8905 PORTLAND ME

POSTAGE WILL BE PAID BY THE ADDRESSEE

MAGIC ATTIC CLUB
866 SPRING ST
PO BOX 9712
PORTLAND ME   04104-9954